30 clearly annotated qu ... ks.

Perfect for ...

THE COMPLETE GUIDE TO DR JEKYLL AND MR HYDE QUOTES

LAURA MCQUIGGIN

The Complete Guide to Dr Jekyll and Mr Hyde Quotes by Laura McQuiggin

www.englishtuitiononline.co.uk

First paperback edition February 2023

Cover, and internal design by Laura McQuiggin
Excerpts taken from *'The Strange Case of Dr Jekyll and Mr Hyde'* by Robert Louis Stevenson

TABLE OF CONTENTS

Introduction

The Quotes

Practice

Conclusion

FOREWORD

As a tutor, I have taught over 2000 lessons. In those lessons, I have learnt a lot about how students approach their English GCSE examinations. Most students who find English trickier tend to have more of an affinity for the more 'logical' subjects, like Maths and Science. In response to this, I have devised a system by which a more formulaic approach can be taken to English GCSE questions. The theory behind this guide is that, if you revise the information it contains, you can apply it in a systematic way to an essay and ensure you hit all the assessment objectives. Additionally, there are several blank worksheets to help you to revise your own selection of quotes.

This guide breaks down 30 key quotations from Dr Jeykll and Mr Hyde into simple, analytical points, which are easy to understand and build on. Each quotation also has relevant context included and applied to the specific quote. Furthermore, links to relevant moments in the play are included to help develop analysis and provide suggestions as to other points that may be made.

The themes of each quotation are included to enable the guide to be used quickly and easily for practice essays. These themes can also encourage the user to consider the quote from multiple angles - a key part of high-level analysis.

Lastly, each quote contains a short summary of what just happened to add clarity to where the quote has come from. This is especially useful for students who aren't yet confident with the plot.

I hope you find this guide useful - if you do have any questions about the contents, please contact me through my website: www.englishtuitiononline.co.uk

LAURA MCQUIGGIN

HOW TO USE THIS BOOK

THIS SECTION TELLS YOU WHAT THEMES AND CHARACTER QUESTIONS THE QUOTE WILL BEST RELATE TO

THIS SECTION GIVES A SUMMARY OF WHAT HAPPENED BEFORE THE QUOTATION AND IS USEFUL TO ENSURE THAT THE QUOTE IS USED CORRECTLY

THEMES / CHARACTERS

Hyde
Enfield
Good vs Evil
Supernatural
Deformity
Violence

SUMMARY

Utterson and Mr Enfield, his friend and cousin, were going on their usual Sunday walk through Soho. Enfield was telling Utterson about a bizarre and horrific incident that he had witnessed in the area. He had seen a strange, repulsive man attack and trample a child.

This plays on the emotions of the reader

The theme of duality is already present in Hyde's character

Connotes youth, vulnerability and innocence

Juxtaposition

Noun

HERE YOU CAN FIND THE QUOTATION, THE TECHNIQUES USED AND A VARIETY OF POTENTIAL POINTS OF ANALYSIS THAT WILL HELP YOU FUFIL AO2

TRAMPLED CALMLY OVER THE CHILD'S BODY

An unusual choice of adverb for the context

We don't know any information about the gender or age of the child

Emphasises the bizarre nature of Hyde, as he has the ability to be both calm and violent at the same time

Perhaps Stevenson deliberately left the physical description of the child vague in order to encourage readers to imagine and emotionally connect with the character

THE ACT, SCENE NUMBER AND WHO SAYS THE QUOTE IS LISTED HERE

ENFIELD - CHAPTER 1

LINKS

Hyde is presented in this quote as oddly calm; however, as the novella progresses, he is depicted as more anxious and furtive. One example of this is his avoidance of eye contact when confronted by Utterson at the back of Jekyll's house. It could be inferred that Hyde is only calm when he is indulging in his violent desires.

CONTEXT

Children are often used in Gothic literature to evoke a sense of empathy in the reader and to demonstrate the 'evilness' of the monster. In *Dracula*, the vampires often targeted children, and in *Frankenstein*, the creature accidentally killed a child. The more recent *The Woman in Black* used a child's cry to create tension. Here, Stevenson uses a child to make the attack seem senseless and to heighten the sense of Hyde's cruelty.

13

THIS SECTION WILL HELP YOU EXPAND YOUR PARAGRAPHS AND MAKE REFERENCES TO THE PLAY AS A WHOLE. THIS CAN ALSO HELP WITH DEPTH OF ANALYSIS

THIS SECTION COVERS A03 AND PROVIDES EXAMPLES OF RELEVANT CONTEXTUAL INFOMATION. MAKE SURE YOU EXPLAIN HOW THIS LINKS TO THE QUOTATION!

HOW TO REVISE JEKYLL AND HYDE

UNDERSTAND THE TEXT

The first thing to do is read the text. Then read it again. Try to read the full text as much as possible before the exam. The more familiar you are with it, the easier it will be to write a top mark essay! If you aren't keen on reading try listening to an unabridged audiobook: it is just as good!

WATCH ADAPTATIONS

Watching productions of the play is a useful way to recap the key scenes and plot points. It is also useful to see the different ways in which the same scene can be interpreted and portrayed. Try to watch as many different versions as possible.

MAKE NOTES ON THE KEY PLOT POINTS

Make notes on the key scenes so you have a clear summary of the plot. This will be useful to refer to when you begin writing essays, and will be a good resource for revision.

PICK THE BEST QUOTES TO LEARN

This is where 'The Complete Guide to Dr Jekyll and Mr Hyde Quotes' comes in! Look through these quotes and pick the ones you feel most confident writing about. It is also worth picking some of your own quotes and preparing them in the same way as is set out in this book. Then start to learn them. It is better to start the learning process as early as possible rather than leaving it to the last minute.

PRACTICE ESSAY QUESTIONS

Practice using the quotes you have learnt to answer essay questions. These can be essays that you have been set at school or ones that you have found online or in this book. Practice makes perfect. It's cliché but it's true! Top tip: if you are short on time, pick an essay question and just practice planning it under timed conditions so you know how you'd structure your essay in the exam.

HOW TO FORMAT QUOTATIONS

SINGLE OR DOUBLE QUOTATION MARKS

You can use either single or double quotation marks. It doesn't matter which. The main thing is that you are consistent. So, whichever you pick, make sure you stick to it!

SHORT OR LONG QUOTES

You don't get marks for the quotes themselves so it's best to stick to shorter quotes. That way you can get straight into the analysis that will get you the marks.

SQUARE BRACKETS

When you change something in a quote you should place it in square brackets to demonstrate that a change has been made.

(Story of the Door)
"He was austere with himself"

"[Mr Utterson] was austere with himself"

ELLIPSE

Ellipses can be used to signify information has been removed from a quote. It is a useful way to break longer quotes down into more manageable chunks.

(Search for Mr Hyde)
"By all lights and at all hours of solitude or concourse, the lawyer was to be found on his chosen post."

"By all lights [...] the lawyer was to be found on his chosen post."

THE ASSESSMENT OBJECTIVES

The assessment objectives are the same for GCSE English Literature across all the exam boards. However, the weighting of marks allotted to each objective does vary. Generally, AO1 and AO2 take up the largest part of the mark scheme. To check the weighting, look on your exam board's website.

AO1 - WRITING STYLE

Read, understand and respond to texts.
Students should be able to: maintain a critical style and develop an informed personal response, use textual references, including quotations, to support and illustrate interpretations.

AO2 - ANALYSIS

Analyse the language, form and structure used by a writer to create meanings and effects, using relevant subject terminology where appropriate.

AO3 - CONTEXT

Show understanding of the relationships between texts and the contexts in which they were written.

AO4 - SPAG

Use a range of vocabulary and sentence structures for clarity, purpose and effect, with accurate spelling and punctuation.

THE QUOTES

PLEASE NOTE:

These quotations are intended to supplement revision and are not an exhaustive list of quotes. The analysis provided offers some potential viewpoints to explore and is not comprehensive.

THEMES / CHARACTERS

Utterson
Friendship
Reputation
Good vs Evil
Religion

SUMMARY

The chapter opens with a description of Mr Utterson, the narrator and central character of the novella. Utterson's character is presented as a likeable, wealthy lawyer, and we learn that he is typically the "last good influence in the lives of down-going men".

Foreshadows Utterson's involvement in Jekyll's complicated and dangerous relationship with Hyde

This phrase suggests that Utterson doesn't attempt to avoid extreme situations

He wants to be of assistance to his friends and doesn't like to criticise them

Demonstrates Utterson's kind nature

IN ANY EXTREMITY INCLINED TO HELP RATHER THAN TO REPROVE. 'I INCLINE TO CAIN'S HERESY,' HE USED TO SAY QUAINTLY: 'I LET MY BROTHER GO TO THE DEVIL IN HIS OWN WAY'.

Dialogue

Draws attention and adds emphasis to what Utterson used to say

Noun

Strong negative connotations

Contrasts with the casual manner in which Utterson is speaking

'Quaint' means something pleasingly unusual or old-fashioned

Encourages the reader to like Utterson

UTTERSON - CHAPTER 1

LINKS

This attitude is reflected in Utterson's later concern for Jekyll. He never looks down on Jekyll for his involvement with Hyde; he simply seeks to support and protect his friend. This tactic ultimately is ineffective in actually helping Jekyll and preventing his downfall.

CONTEXT

The reference to "Cain's Heresy" alludes to the biblical story of Adam and Eve's sons, Cain and Abel. Cain felt that God preferred Abel's sacrifices so he murdered his brother. Some see Cain as the origin of evil, while his brother, Abel, is a symbol of goodness. This echoes the theme of duality, which is present throughout the text.

THEMES / CHARACTERS

Hyde
Enfield
Good vs Evil
Supernatural
Deformity
Violence

SUMMARY

Utterson and Mr Enfield, his friend and cousin, were going on their usual Sunday walk through Soho. Enfield was telling Utterson about a bizarre and horrific incident that he had witnessed in the area. He had seen a strange, repulsive man attack and trample a child.

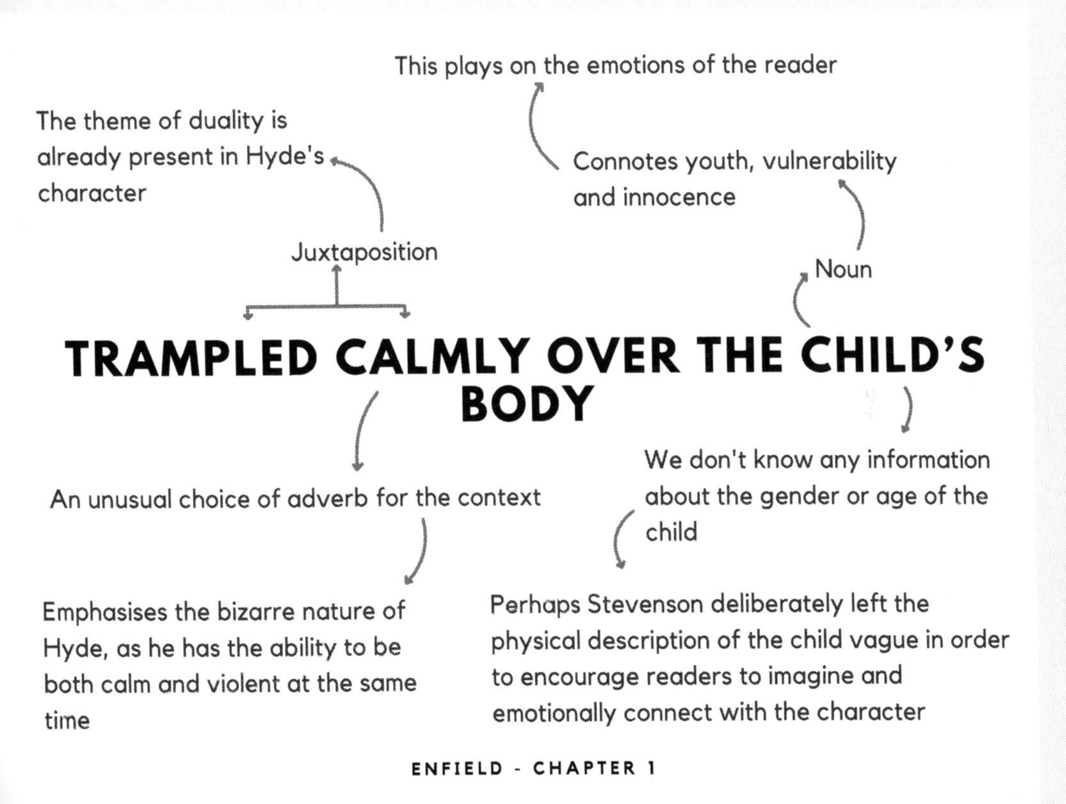

ENFIELD - CHAPTER 1

LINKS

Hyde is presented in this quote as oddly calm; however, as the novella progresses, he is depicted as more anxious and furtive. One example of this is his avoidance of eye contact when confronted by Utterson at the back of Jekyll's house. It could be inferred that Hyde is only calm when he is indulging in his violent desires.

CONTEXT

Children are often used in Gothic literature to evoke a sense of empathy in the reader and to demonstrate the 'evilness' of the monster. In *Dracula*, the vampires often targeted children, and in *Frankenstein*, the creature accidentally killed a child. The more recent *The Woman in Black* used a child's cry to create tension. Here, Stevenson uses a child to make the attack seem senseless and to heighten the sense of Hyde's cruelty.

THEMES / CHARACTERS

Hyde
Enfield
Good vs Evil
Supernatural
Deformity
Suspicion

SUMMARY

Enfield was telling Utterson about the attack. He spoke of how the child's parents and a doctor had all rushed to help the child, and how they were disgusted by the evilness of the attacker, Hyde. Enfield described the perpetrator's behaviour.

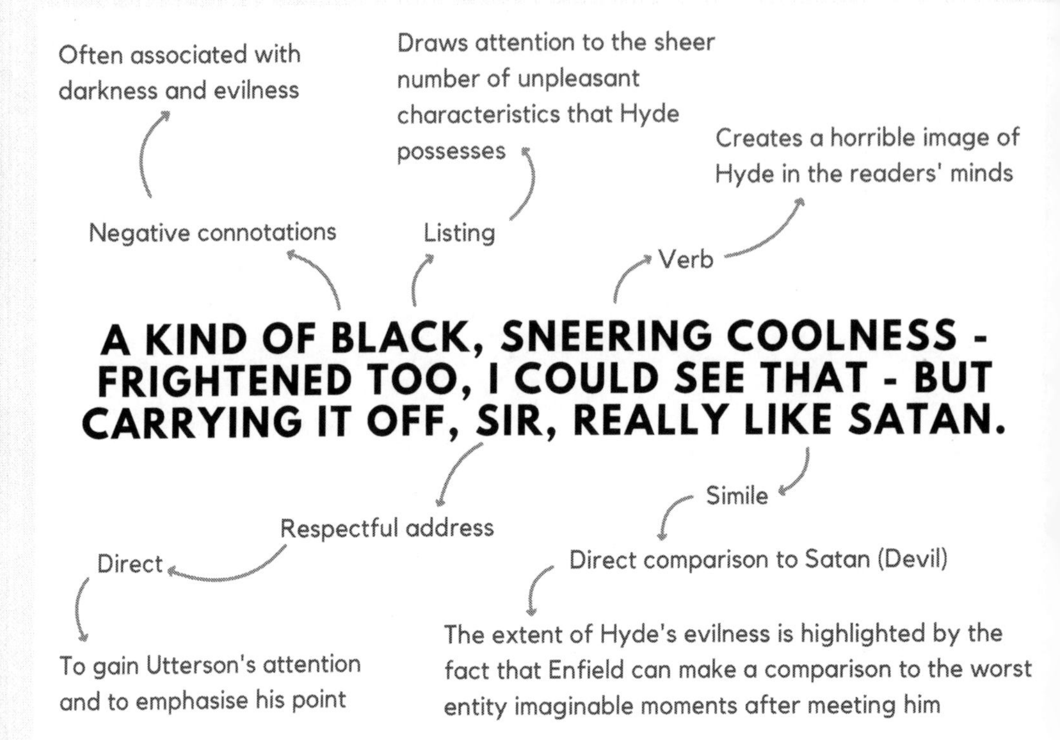

ENFIELD - CHAPTER 1

LINKS

The antithesis between Hyde's being "frightened" but maintaining "coolness" reflects the duality that is present throughout the novella and is reminiscent of the juxtaposition of his "trampling calmly" in the previous quote.

CONTEXT

In Victorian times, the majority of the population would have been Christian and would have had a good knowledge of the Bible. The reference to "Satan" would be understood by the readers, who would have seen the Devil as a very real and dangerous being.

THEMES / CHARACTERS

Jekyll
Enfield
Reputation
Societal expectations
Good vs Evil
Suspicion

SUMMARY

Enfield continued to tell the story. He explained that the family wanted compensation for the attack. The man, called Mr Hyde, agreed to give them money. Hyde went into a nearby house and came out with a cheque for £100, signed by a wealthy and prestigious man whom Enfield refused to name (Jekyll).

He is perceived this way by Enfield, who is not directly acquainted with him. This makes Enfield's comments seem impartial and thus we are compelled to believe in the goodness of Jekyll

Highlights Jekyll's good reputation to the reader

Means 'paying an excessive amount for something'

Idiom

Adjective - referring to Jekyll

AN HONEST MAN PAYING THROUGH THE NOSE FOR SOME OF THE CAPERS OF HIS YOUTH

In this context meaning 'illicit or risky activities'

Euphemism

Suggests that these "capers" only occurred when Jekyll was young

Could imply that Enfield believes Jekyll has engaged in homosexuality, or other contextually unacceptable activities

We can infer that Enfield holds sympathy for Jekyll despite his connection to Hyde

ENFIELD - CHAPTER 1

LINKS

Utterson later says something similar, claiming Jekyll "was wild when he was young" and that Hyde must be "the ghost of some old sin, the cancer of some concealed disgrace."

Suggestions of homosexuality are also shown when Jekyll wakes up in his own house as Hyde. He has to wear Jekyll's clothes, which are too large, and walk out of the house. The servants, seeing this, would have thought Hyde had stayed the night with Jekyll.

CONTEXT

In Victorian society, wealthy upper-class men were at the top of the power hierarchy. Occasionally, they would do things that were not socially acceptable, such as having affairs, siring illegitimate children, and engaging in homosexuality. These things were looked down upon and considered deeply shameful in public life. Enfield suggests here that Hyde is trying to blackmail Jekyll with some sort of scandal from when Jekyll was younger.

THEMES / CHARACTERS

Lanyon
Jekyll
Friendship
Science
Reputation
Religion

SUMMARY

Utterson asked Dr Lanyon if he had seen Jekyll recently. Lanyon explained that their friendship had taken a downturn, as they had had a strong disagreement about scientific matters.

Could allude to the bad path Jekyll has gone down

Stevenson could be emphasising the strained relationship between them

"Devilish" evokes negative connotations

Does not refer to Jekyll by name

I HAVE SEEN DEVILISH LITTLE OF THE MAN. SUCH UNSCIENTIFIC BALDERDASH

Shows that he does not believe what Jekyll has spoken of to be 'real' science

Also reveals how passionate Lanyon is about following 'proper' science in comparison to Jekyll's foray into dark science

Colloquial language

Means 'nonsense'

Insulting towards Jekyll and his ideas - again reinforces the strained nature of their relationship

LANYON - CHAPTER 2

LINKS

Alludes to a previous disagreement regarding science and foreshadows further differences between the doctors.

Shows the strained relationship between Lanyon and Jekyll, who were once close friends. Suggests that the difference in scientific judgement must have been very great to cause such a rift in their friendship.

CONTEXT

The Industrial Revolution rapidly changed the way things were done. There was a renewed interest in science and technology, and how it could improve people's lives. Some people disliked how quickly elements of society were transforming and tried to resist those changes. Lanyon could be seen to be reluctant to explore new avenues of science. Equally, Jekyll's fate could serve as a warning not to try to push the boundaries of science too far.

THEMES / CHARACTERS

Hyde
Good vs Evil
Religion
Supernatural
Deformity
Societal expectations
Suspicion

SUMMARY

Utterson, hearing of the horrors of Hyde and concerned that his friend Jekyll could be involved with such a man, spiralled into a fit of suspicion. He decided to wait outside the place where Hyde was living. When he saw Hyde, he approached him.

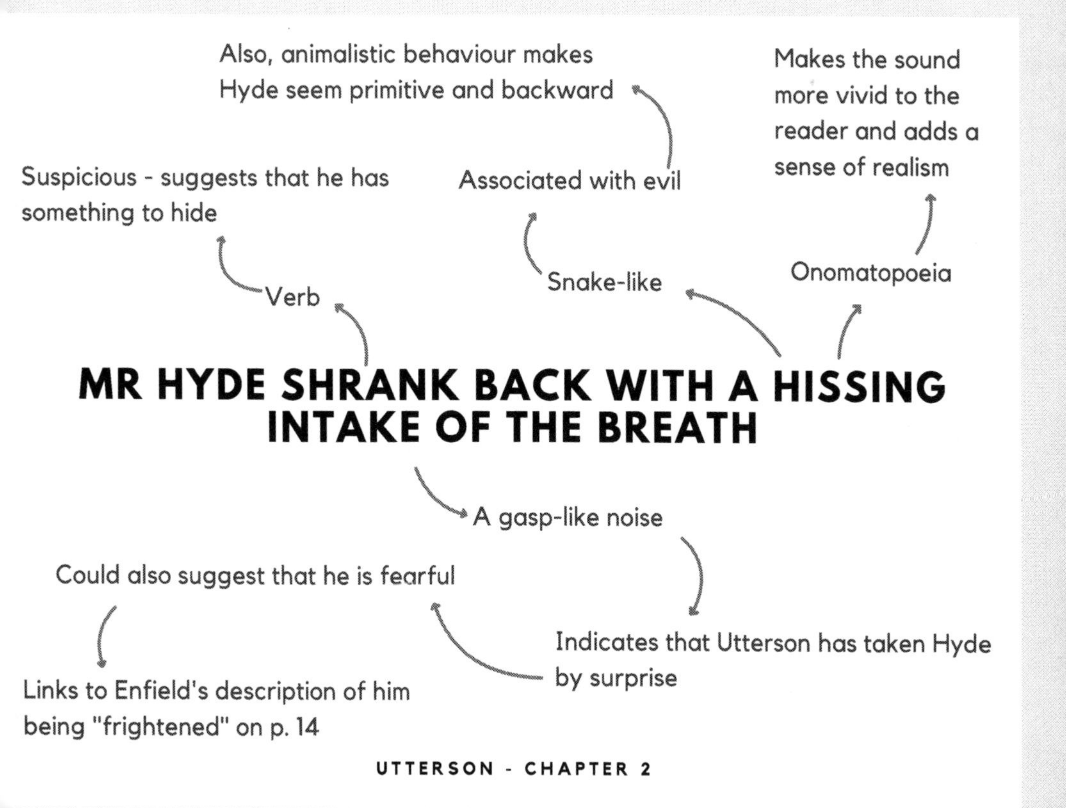

LINKS

Links to the other animalistic descriptions of Hyde (p. 22, 32).

The secretive nature of Hyde encourages Utterson's suspicion, which leads him to press Jekyll for more information about his relationship with Hyde.

CONTEXT

Readers at the time would have been familiar with the biblical story of Adam and Eve. Eve, the first woman, was convinced to eat the forbidden fruit by an evil serpent. As punishment, God cursed humanity to mortality and cursed the snake to have to move on its belly. This famous story has influenced the usage of snakes and snake-like characteristics in literature. The hissing here connotes the evilness of the snake in the Garden of Eden.

THEMES / CHARACTERS

Hyde
Utterson
Supernatural
Good vs Evil
Deformity
Societal expectations
Suspicion

SUMMARY

Utterson had been speaking with Hyde when Hyde asked how Utterson knew him. Utterson said they had "common friends," such as "Jekyll, for instance." Hyde accused him of lying and disappeared into his house, leaving Utterson shocked. Utterson tried to express what was wrong with Hyde's character.

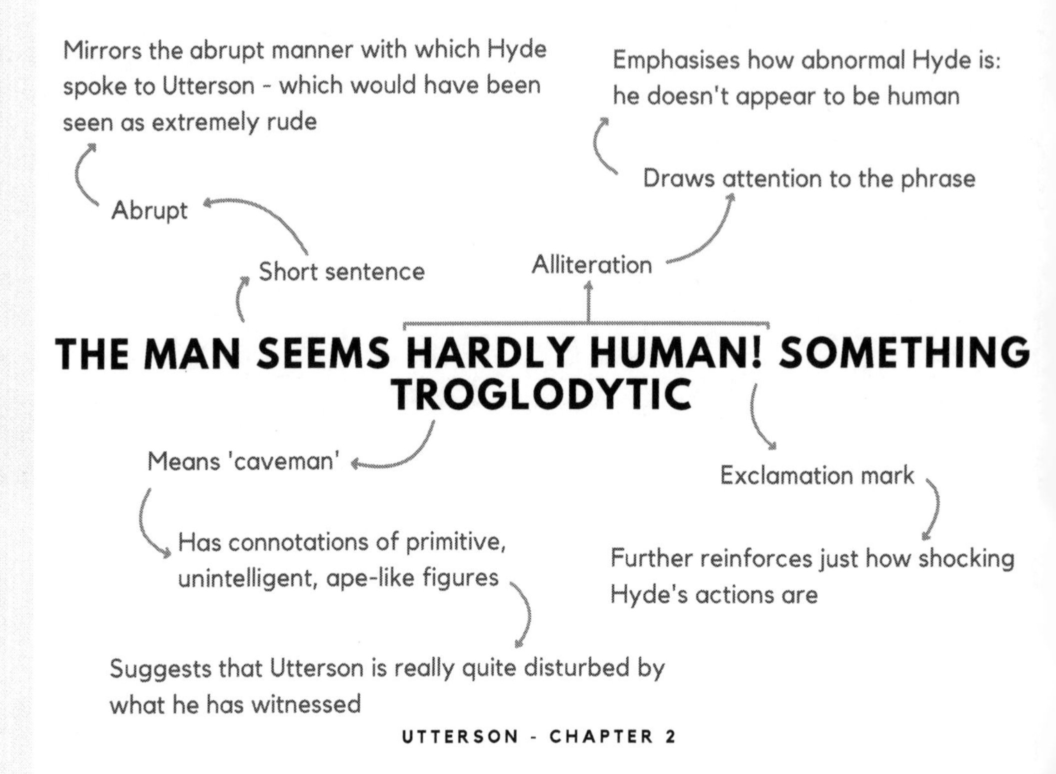

UTTERSON - CHAPTER 2

LINKS

Again presenting Hyde as sub-human and animalistic.

The reference to "troglodytic" suggests that there is something primordial about Hyde, which is supported in the later descriptions of him being "ape-like" and having "a swarthy growth of hair" on his hand.

CONTEXT

Charles Darwin offered theories such as evolution and natural selection which went against the religious belief that God had created everything (creationism). This reference to Hyde being "troglodytic", meaning that he is caveman-like and primitive, could be a reference to Darwin's theories - that actually we are descended from apes rather than divine creations.

THEMES / CHARACTERS

Jekyll
Utterson
Friendship
Reputation
Curiosity

SUMMARY

Utterson was concerned by Jekyll's association with Hyde, and frustrated that Jekyll had named Hyde in his will. Utterson decided to question Jekyll on the nature of their relationship. Jekyll was very elusive and, despite trusting Utterson, refused to explain the situation fully.

The exaggeration could suggest that Jekyll is lying or being deceptive

Exaggerating for dramatic effect - perhaps Jekyll is trying to be more persuasive to encourage Utterson to drop the matter

Contrast with what is he saying - if he actually trusted Utterson, why would he be so secretive?

Hyperbole

I WOULD TRUST YOU BEFORE ANY MAN ALIVE, AY BEFORE MYSELF

Colloquial language

Irony

Makes his words seem spontaneous and truthful

Reveals his sincerity

Jekyll trusts himself to have control over his transformations into Hyde, and when he does start to face issues, he chooses Lanyon to confide in. This suggests he does not trust Utterson as much as he claims

JEKYLL - CHAPTER 3

LINKS

This is later proven to be untrue. Hyde is part of Jekyll, and so Jekyll's decision to continue his transformations and remain associated with Hyde demonstrates that he trusts his own judgement the most.

Jekyll left Utterson a letter explaining the entire situation, including his own thoughts and feelings about the transformations, before committing suicide. This suggests that he did trust Utterson.

CONTEXT

Male friendships during the Victorian era were characterized by an intense sentimentality, with deeply held feelings and emotions. This was partly attributed to the limited or restricted interaction between members of the opposite gender. Consequently, male-male friendships were highly valued and cherished, offering companionship and a sense of understanding. This quote reflects the profound relationship between Utterson and Jekyll.

THEMES / CHARACTERS

Jekyll
Good vs Evil
Reputation
Deception
Suspicion

SUMMARY

Jekyll continues to evade Utterson's constant questioning. Utterson worries that his friend is being blackmailed. Jekyll denies this and claims that he is able to break off his friendship with Hyde whenever he desires.

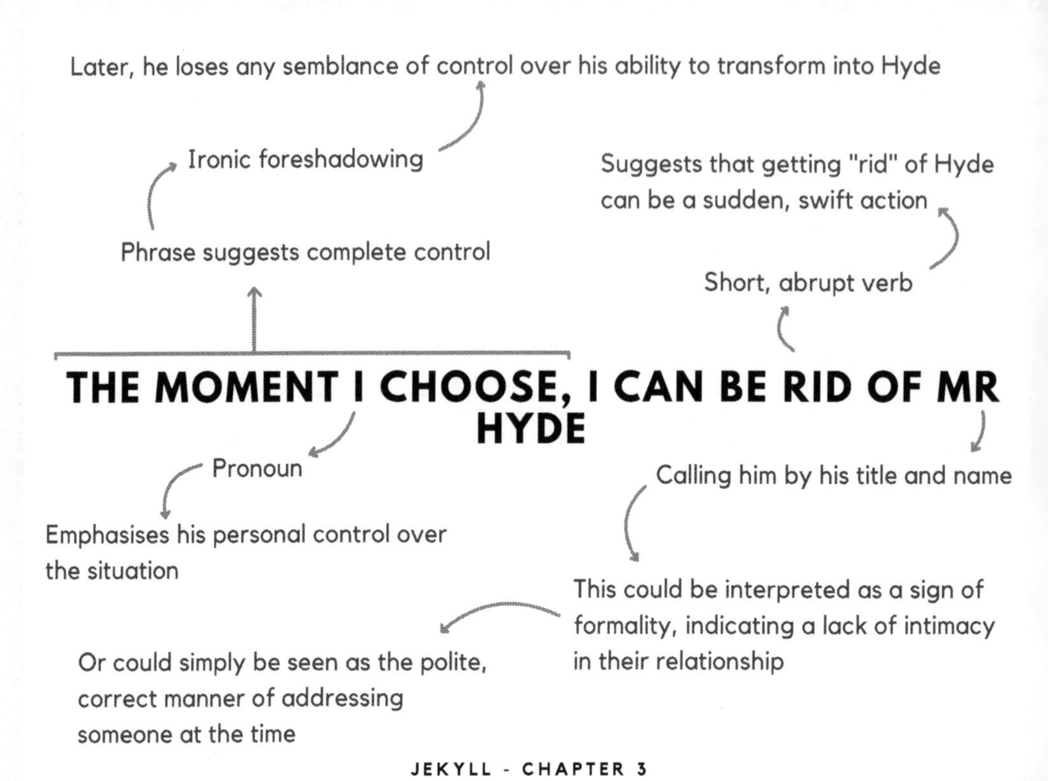

JEKYLL - CHAPTER 3

LINKS

This foreshadows the end of the novella where Jekyll realises that he can no longer choose when he transforms into Hyde, and therefore cannot be "rid of" him. This quote implies that Jekyll thought he could commit evil acts through the persona of Hyde without any repercussions.

CONTEXT

Calvinism, the religion that Stevenson grew up with, required followers to achieve perfection: to be completely good and without fault. Jekyll's decision to transform into another being so he can indulge in sinful activities suggests that Stevenson felt that perfection was unobtainable; individuals would always be tempted by the desire to let their darker side take over.

THEMES / CHARACTERS

Hyde
Violence
Good vs Evil
Reputation
Supernatural
Setting

SUMMARY

A maid, looking out of her window one evening, saw Sir Danvers Carew walking through the street. He was suddenly killed in a frenzied attack by a strange man, who was later discovered to be Mr Hyde.

We are told that a "crime" has occurred to a high-ranking person; however, the precise details are delayed, creating tension and interest as we wait to see what has happened

Has connotations of surprise and fear

Ambiguous

Adds emphasis to the violent nature of the crime

STARTLED BY A CRIME OF SINGULAR FEROCITY AND RENDERED ALL THE MORE NOTABLE BY THE HIGH POSITION OF THE VICTIM

Reveals that the victim was of the upper classes

Reinforces the importance of the class system that divided the Victorian era

The use of "notable" indicates that the crime was seen to be more important due to the high status of the individual

UTTERSON - CHAPTER 4

LINKS

The emphasis on the "high position of the victim" links to the theme of reputation, which occurs throughout the novella.

The maid who witnessed the murder describes Sir Danvers Carew as having an "innocent and old-world kindness of disposition." This description links to the first attack on the child. Stevenson presents both victims as "innocents," which emphasises the cruelty of the attacks.

CONTEXT

In Victorian society, social classes were clearly defined and those in the upper classes were keen to ensure they remained at the top. There would have been a sense that the upper classes were untouchable. The murder of Sir Danvers Carew, a wealthy, titled, upper-class man, would have been particularly shocking for this reason.

THEMES / CHARACTERS

Hyde
Violence
Deformity
Good vs Evil
Supernatural

SUMMARY

The maid who witnessed the murder of Sir Danvers Carew describes what she saw in vivid detail. She explains how the assault was so violent that "the bones were audibly shattered, and the body jumped upon the roadway".

The comparisons to an animal make Hyde appear uncontrollable, unreasonable and unpredictable

Again emphasising how unfair the attack was

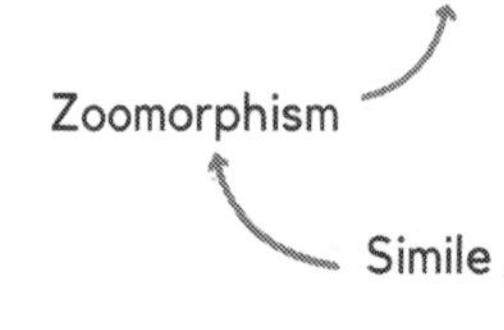

Suggests that he completely overpowered Sir Danvers

Heavy-sounding verb

WITH, APE-LIKE FURY, HE WAS TRAMPING HIS VICTIM UNDER FOOT, AND HAILING DOWN A STORM OF BLOWS

"Under foot" indicates that Hyde is not fighting fair

Metaphor

This is not a mutual fight where both opponents are on an equal footing. Hyde is using the 'upper hand' of having Sir Danvers beneath him to be even more violent

Suggests the frequency and violence of the punches Hyde was throwing

UTTERSON - CHAPTER 4

LINKS

Links to the quotes that depict Hyde as animalistic (p. 17, 32).

The extreme, unexpected and unprovoked violence here is reminiscent of the initial attack on the child, described by Enfield in Chapter 1. Hyde does not appear to have any motive behind his attacks other than indulging in violence.

CONTEXT

The upper-class Victorians led privileged lives, sheltered from the realities of the working class. They were expected to behave with propriety, and physical confrontation was strongly discouraged. Consequently, acts of violence were rarely seen in public society, which may explain why Mr Hyde seems to take pleasure in them – it was an aberration of the norms of the day.

THEMES / CHARACTERS

Utterson
Setting
Good vs Evil
Supernatural
Deformity

SUMMARY

After learning that the murderer of Sir Danvers Carew is Mr Hyde, Utterson offered to help the police by taking them to Hyde's house. They travelled through the "dismal quarter of Soho" at nine in the morning.

Adjective "mournful" shows how even the environment has become miserable

Personification

Literally indicating the darkness of the night, but could also metaphorically symbolise the darkness of Hyde

Strong negative connotations

MOURNFUL REINVASION OF DARKNESS SEEMED, IN THE LAWYER'S EYES, LIKE A DISTRICT OF SOME CITY IN A NIGHTMARE.

Draws attention to the city landscape

Cities often have connotations of liveliness, but London seems desolate and eerie in this description

Simile

Comparison to a nightmare continues the negative depiction of the environment of London

UTTERSON - CHAPTER 4

LINKS

Links to other descriptions of the setting:

"[S]treet after street, all lighted up as if for a procession and all as empty as a church".

"It was a wild, cold seasonable night of March".

"Fog slept above the drowned city".

"[B]ore in every feature, the marks of prolonged and sordid negligence."

CONTEXT

Gothic novels are often set in isolated places to create a sense of unease. Stevenson breaks away from this trope by setting the story in a city, London. Despite the busy nature of a city, Stevenson focuses on small moments of isolation by describing the empty backstreets of London at night. "Street after street, and all the folks asleep," when a man "begins to long for the sight of a policeman."

THEMES / CHARACTERS

Hyde
Deformity
Supernatural
Good vs Evil
Curiosity

SUMMARY

The police attempted to capture Hyde, but were unsuccessful. They continued to search for him, but found people's descriptions of Hyde "differed widely". Nonetheless, they all noticed his "haunting sense of unexpressed deformity".

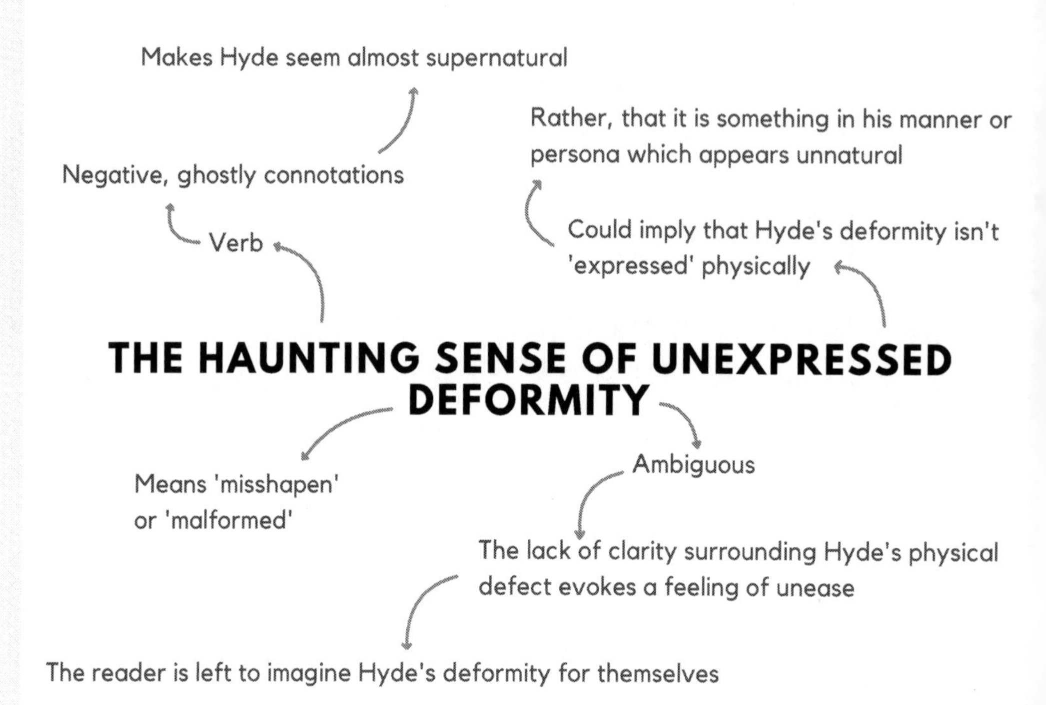

UTTERSON - CHAPTER 4

LINKS

Links to several quotes that depict Hyde as deformed. "[H]e gives a strong feeling of deformity", "he gave the impression of deformity" and "left on that body an imprint of deformity and decay". We are told that Hyde is 'dwarfish' and ugly, yet we never find out exactly what is causing everyone to describe him as deformed. The use of "sense", "feeling", and "impression" suggest that the deformity is intangible.

CONTEXT

Victorians had a keen interest in the supernatural. Their lives were often restrictive, so the supernatural allowed them an avenue to consider and explore wild, fantastical ideas such as vampires, ghosts and monsters. The repeated references to deformity are reminiscent of other supernatural, deformed entities, such as The Creature from Mary Shelley's novel *Frankenstein*.

THEMES / CHARACTERS

Jekyll
Friendship
Reputation
Societal expectations
Deception
Good vs Evil

SUMMARY

Utterson had gone to speak to Jekyll about the murder. Jekyll was horrified and renounced Hyde. He claimed Hyde had sent him a letter. He was unsure about taking the letter to the police, as involvement with Hyde could damage his reputation.

He has had to sacrifice his interest in Hyde to maintain his public persona as a respectable individual

Suggests that Jekyll is finally thinking clearly without the influence of Hyde

Shows the importance of reputation

Pronoun

Focusing on himself

I WAS THINKING OF MY OWN CHARACTER, WHICH THIS HATEFUL BUSINESS HAS RATHER EXPOSED

Adjective

Shows a passion we haven't seen from Jekyll before

Previously, he had been very private about his feelings towards Hyde and, while defensive, he never expressed any negative emotions towards Hyde

JEKYLL - CHAPTER 5

LINKS

This contrasts with Jekyll's previous behaviour. He has always defended his relationship with Hyde.

Part of the reason for the transformation is to allow Jekyll to indulge in his darker side without it affecting his reputation. If he is linked to Hyde, then it could ruin his public image.

CONTEXT

John Hunter was an upper-class doctor who many believe inspired Stevenson's presentation of Jekyll. Grave robbers would bring bodies to the back of Hunter's house in Leicester Square for him to experiment on. Hunter dissected these bodies in the pursuit of science, to better understand anatomy. The moral cost of using bodies without permission, for the pursuit of scientific knowledge, mimics the moral complexities of Jekyll's situation.

THEMES / CHARACTERS

Utterson
Friendship
Curiosity
Suspicion
Deception

SUMMARY

Utterson, upon hearing that Jekyll had nothing to do with the murder of Sir Danvers Carew and that Hyde had left the area, felt relieved. He gently chastised himself for his previous suspicions.

He doubts himself - despite the fact Jekyll was behaving oddly, and he was right about Hyde being a bad person

Shows Utterson's predisposition to feel guilt

Indicates that he no longer holds these suspicions

HE BLAMED HIMSELF FOR SOME OF HIS PAST SUSPICIONS

Utterson harboured deep suspicions about Hyde, and was dubious of Jekyll's association with him.

Unclear exactly what Utterson's "past suspicions" were

Perhaps he suspected that Hyde and Jekyll were in a homosexual relationship

Or that Hyde was blackmailing Jekyll

UTTERSON - CHAPTER 5

LINKS

Utterson was initially concerned and suspicious when he read Jekyll's will. The will stated that in the event of "Dr Jekyll's disappearance" all Jekyll's possessions and money would pass to Mr Hyde.

He had become so suspicious that his dreams were haunted by the "faceless" Mr Hyde.

CONTEXT

The fear of the unknown is a key trope in Gothic literature. Characters become obsessed, yet terrified of mysterious, unknown, supernatural forces at work. Utterson's suspicion of Hyde and his unknown deformity could be an attempt by Stevenson to evoke the Gothic trope to create tension in the text.

THEMES / CHARACTERS

Lanyon
Friendship
Supernatural
Science
Deformity
Suspicion

SUMMARY

Utterson had gone to visit Lanyon. He discovered that Lanyon's health had deteriorated and that he was close to death. Lanyon explained that he had "had a shock" and that he would "never recover", but he refused to tell Utterson the details.

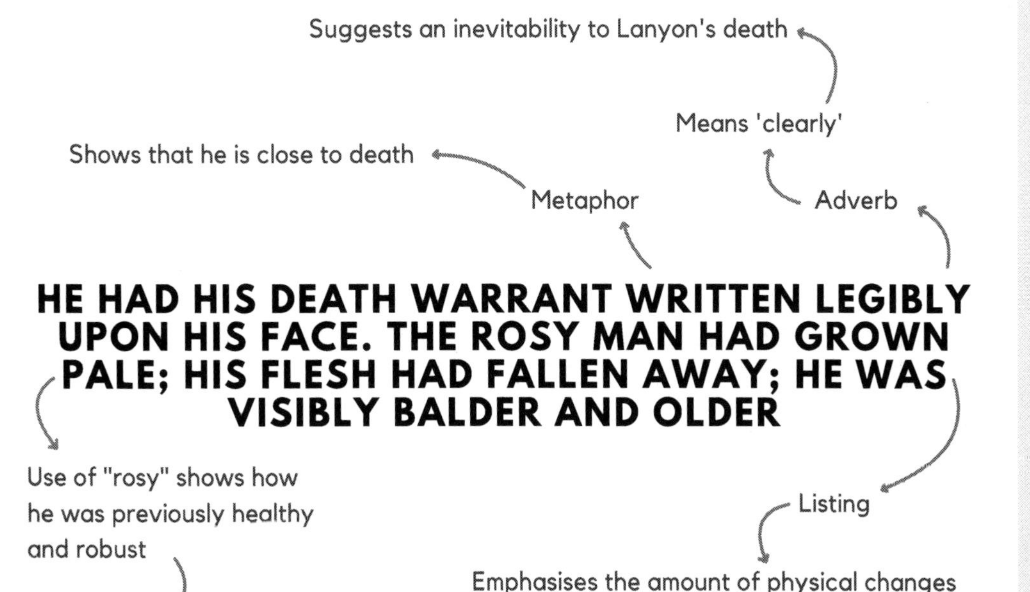

UTTERSON (DESCRIBING LANYON) - CHAPTER 6

LINKS

This contrasts with Lanyon's earlier depiction as being healthy and robust. This deterioration was very sudden.

This transformation is similar to the one Utterson and Enfield witnessed Jekyll going through when they spoke to him through his window. Though the narration does not provide a detailed description of the changes, their reaction indicates that it was a drastic transformation.

CONTEXT

Gothic texts were a reflection of the anxieties of the Victorian era (1837-1901), but also a source of escapism and fascination. People were drawn to the idea of transformation, which was often utilized in the genre. Examples include a dead body being brought to life in Mary Shelley's *Frankenstein* (1818) and the transformation of the innocent and pure Lucy Westenra into a child-killing vampire in Bram Stoker's *Dracula* (1897). Here, we see the robust Dr Lanyon transformed into an invalid.

THEMES / CHARACTERS

Utterson
Friendship
Reputation
Societal expectations
Curiosity
Suspicion

SUMMARY

Lanyon's condition deteriorated quickly, and he was soon dead. After attending Lanyon's funeral, Utterson learned that his friend had left him a letter, with clear instructions to only read it in the event of Jekyll's disappearance.

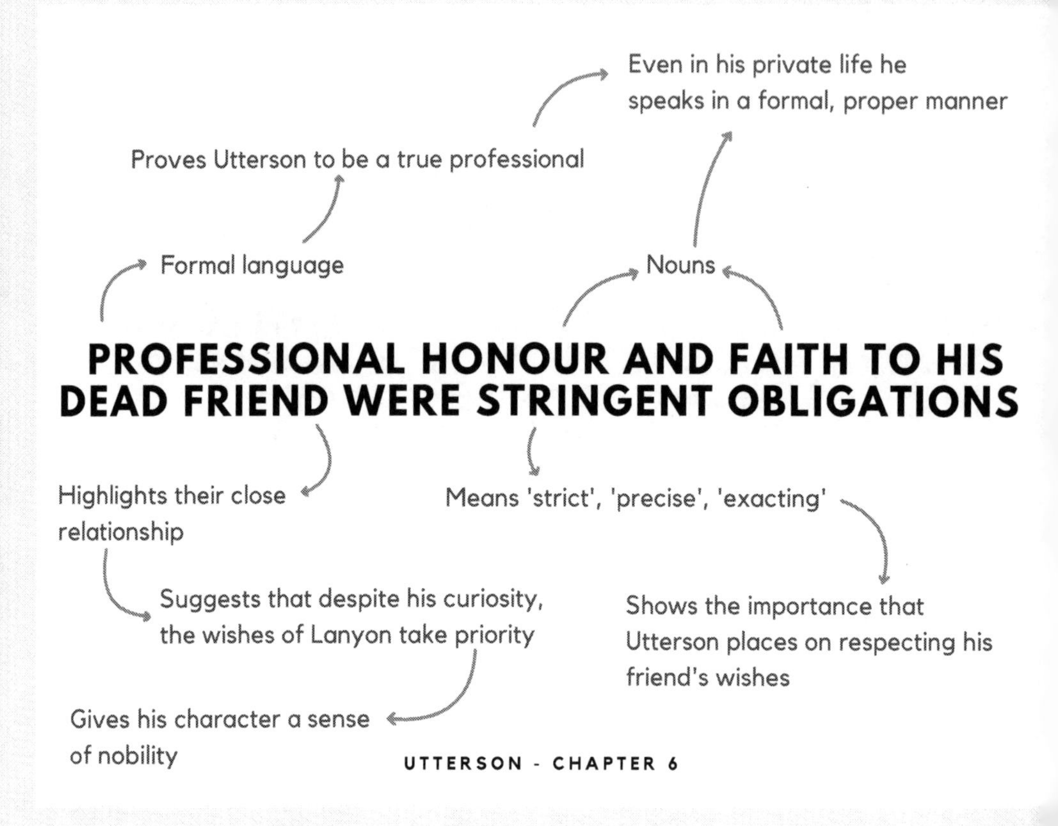

UTTERSON - CHAPTER 6

LINKS

Links to the presentation of Utterson's character throughout the novella. He is consistently determined to be honourable and righteous in his treatment of his friends even when he doesn't understand the reasons behind their unusual behaviour.

CONTEXT

Following social customs was extremely important to the Victorians. Utterson, as a lawyer, was expected to lead by example and uphold the standards of behaviour expected of him. His personal sense of duty is strong, and he is aware that others look to him for guidance and inspiration.

THEMES / CHARACTERS

Jekyll
Supernatural
Deception
Suspicion
Friendship
Setting

SUMMARY

Utterson and Enfield were going on another walk through Soho. As they walked, they spotted Jekyll leaning out of his window, getting some fresh air. They stopped to have a conversation, during which Jekyll revealed that he was not doing very well.

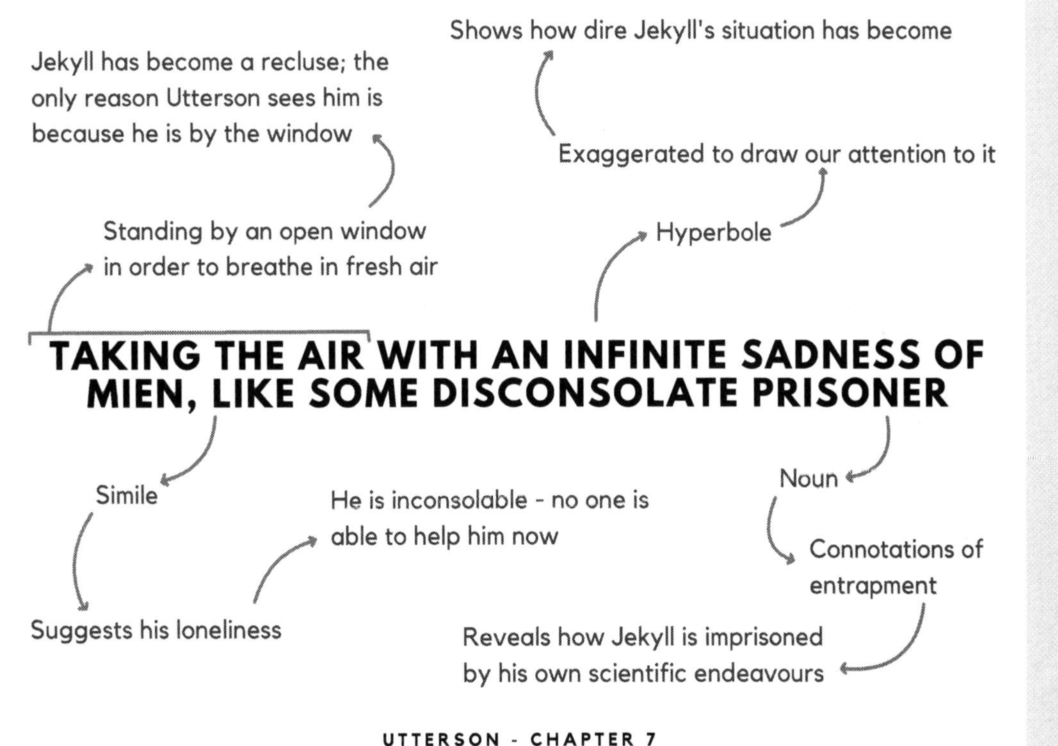

UTTERSON - CHAPTER 7

LINKS

Links to Jekyll's previous letter, which stated that he meant "henceforth to lead a life of extreme seclusion".

Structural link to the beginning of the text where Utterson and Enfield were walking through Soho and went past Jekyll's house.

CONTEXT

The air across London was extremely polluted due to the increased use of factories during the Industrial Revolution. This pollution was exacerbated by poor ventilation and dampness, which could cause serious health issues. Jekyll, with his medical background, would have been aware of the importance of taking in fresh air, especially when confined indoors.

THEMES / CHARACTERS

Jekyll
Utterson
Supernatural
Good vs Evil
Violence
Suspicion

SUMMARY

Utterson and Enfield spoke with Jekyll, who was leaning out of his window. Jekyll seemed to be brightening up at their company. Suddenly, his demeanour changed to horror and he immediately retreated into his house and slammed the window shut. The men, shocked at what they had witnessed, left silently.

The violence here is technically caused by Hyde, as it is the transformation into Hyde that is causing Jekyll distress

Aggressive language is often associated Hyde

Shows he was happy to be speaking with his old friend

Violent verb

THE SMILE WAS STRUCK OUT OF HIS FACE AND SUCCEEDED BY AN EXPRESSION OF SUCH ABJECT TERROR AND DESPAIR, AS FROZE THE VERY BLOOD OF THE TWO GENTLEMEN BELOW

Strong nouns

Creates an atmosphere of fear and suspense

As readers, we are not entirely sure what they have witnessed, which creates further tension

UTTERSON - CHAPTER 7

LINKS

The suddenness of Jekyll's change here mimics Lanyon's abrupt transformation from fit and healthy to fatally ill.

Links to Chapter 10, where we learn that Jekyll had begun to lose control of his transformations.

CONTEXT

Mental health conditions were not widely recognized in the Victorian era. Those who displayed signs of poor mental health were often labelled as mad and either left without any support or sent to insane asylums, which rarely provided effective treatment. Here, Jekyll's odd behaviour could be interpreted as a sign of mental illness.

THEMES / CHARACTERS

Utterson
Poole
Science
Societal expectations
Curiosity

SUMMARY

Poole and the rest of the servants are concerned by their master's odd behaviour. They don't know what to do, so they look to Utterson for help. Utterson dismisses Poole's suggestion that Jekyll has been murdered and the murderer is hiding in Jekyll's room.

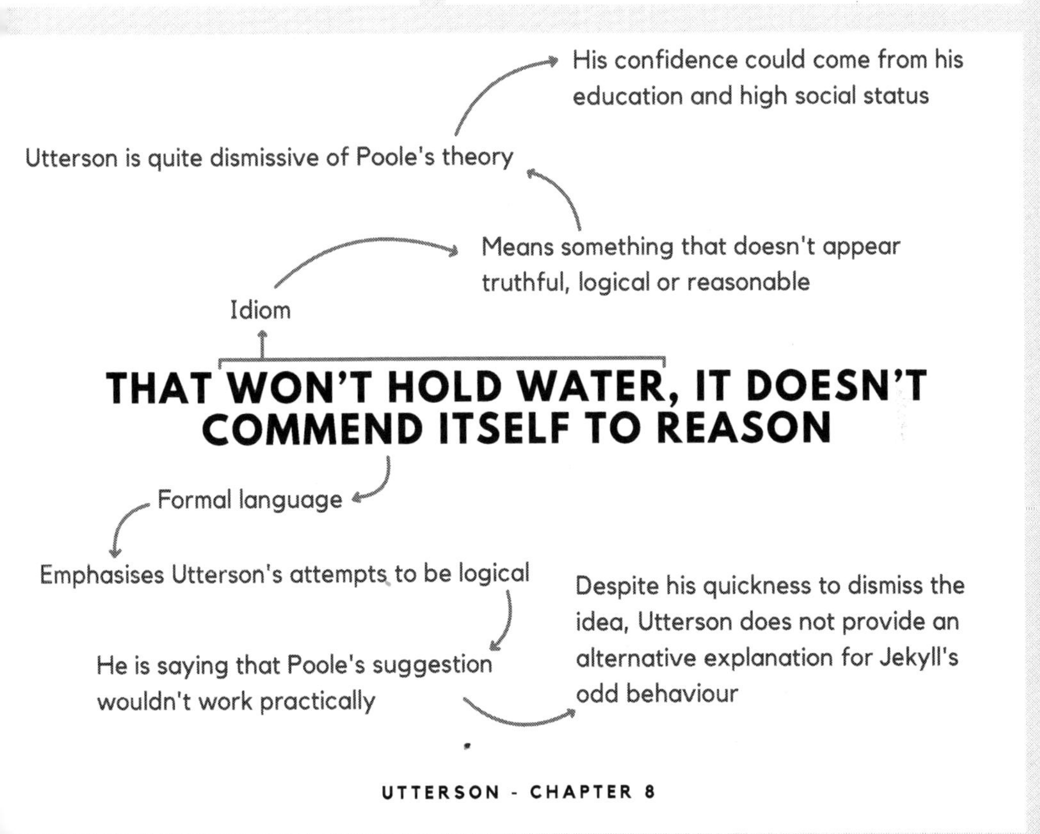

UTTERSON - CHAPTER 8

LINKS

Utterson attempts to be rational and logical throughout the text. His main mistake is trying to rationalise something which is inexplicable - supernatural transformations.

He is heavily influenced by his profession as a lawyer, which emphasises approaching problems in a pragmatic manner.

CONTEXT

In Victorian times, the education of individuals differed greatly based on their class and income. Servants were usually uneducated or left school at a young age to go into service. This resulted in a large educational divide between the upper and lower classes. Utterson assumes that he is more intelligent because he is educated, and uses this to dismiss Poole's suggestion as illogical.

THEMES / CHARACTERS

Jekyll
Hyde
Poole
Reputation
Societal expectations

SUMMARY

Poole is convinced that the man who is hiding in Jekyll's room is not Jekyll. Utterson discredits Poole's notion as absurd. Poole explains that he has worked for Jekyll for a long time and knows his master's voice. He questions why Jekyll would hide from his servant.

Emphasises the hierarchy in the household

"Cry out" indicates fear, but a master would not be afraid of his servants, as they would be considered beneath him

Formal noun

Contrast

IF IT WAS MY MASTER, WHY DID HE CRY OUT LIKE A RAT, AND RUN FROM ME?

Simile

The comparison to a rodent is highly negative

Question

Pushing Utterson to provide a reasonable explanation

Rodents have connotations of a low status, which contrasts with Jekyll's position as master of the house and his high status in wider society

POOLE -CHAPTER 8

LINKS

Links to previous animalistic descriptions of Hyde. Previously he was depicted as having "ape-like" strength, now he is depicted as a rat, a weak rodent.

Ultimately, the servants' decision to reach out to Jekyll's old friend, Utterson, links to the ongoing theme of loyalty. Their duty is to their master, even at his worst.

CONTEXT

Some Victorians, usually those of the upper classes, held idyllic notions of the servant-master relationship. They believed that their servants enjoyed their place in society and idolised their masters. However, given the poor working conditions and treatment of servants, this notion was unlikely. In Stevenson's work, Poole is presented as a loving and devoted servant who admires Dr Jekyll but is unable to understand him.

THEMES / CHARACTERS

Hyde
Jekyll
Societal expectations
Violence
Religion
Deformity

SUMMARY

Utterson decides, after listening to Poole, that something must be wrong with Jekyll. When Utterson knocks on the door, Hyde's voice answers. Utterson decides that the only solution is to break down the door. When he does so, he discovers that Hyde has committed suicide.

This would mean that he could be questioned and brought to justice

Creates momentary excitement in the reader as we think Hyde may be alive

Meaning the muscles in his face

Tells us that Hyde's face is still moving

THE CORDS OF HIS FACE STILL MOVED WITH A SEMBLANCE OF LIFE, BUT LIFE WAS QUITE GONE

A grotesque image of his face twitching as though he was still alive

Conjunction

The use of "quite" adds a sense of certainty, leaving the reader with no doubt

Indicates a change

Revealed that Hyde is in fact dead

UTTERSON - CHAPTER 8

LINKS

Jekyll was previously seen looking dejectedly out of his window. The sadness he was described to have had could be seen to foreshadow his suicide.

Also links to the desperation that he clearly expressed in the letters when he was trying to find the correct drug.

CONTEXT

Victorian society was largely religious and held staunch beliefs about moral righteousness. Suicide was seen as a sin, as only God should decide who lives and who dies. The language used to describe suicide often avoided explicitly stating the act, and there was a sense of shame associated with it. We can see this in the quote.

THEMES / CHARACTERS

Jekyll
Friendship
Good vs Evil
Deception
Reputation
Suspicion

SUMMARY

Lanyon's account reveals that he received an unusual letter from Jekyll. He was told in the letter to go to Jekyll's house, pick up one particular drawer from the cabinet, and bring it back to his own home. An unknown visitor would collect it at midnight.

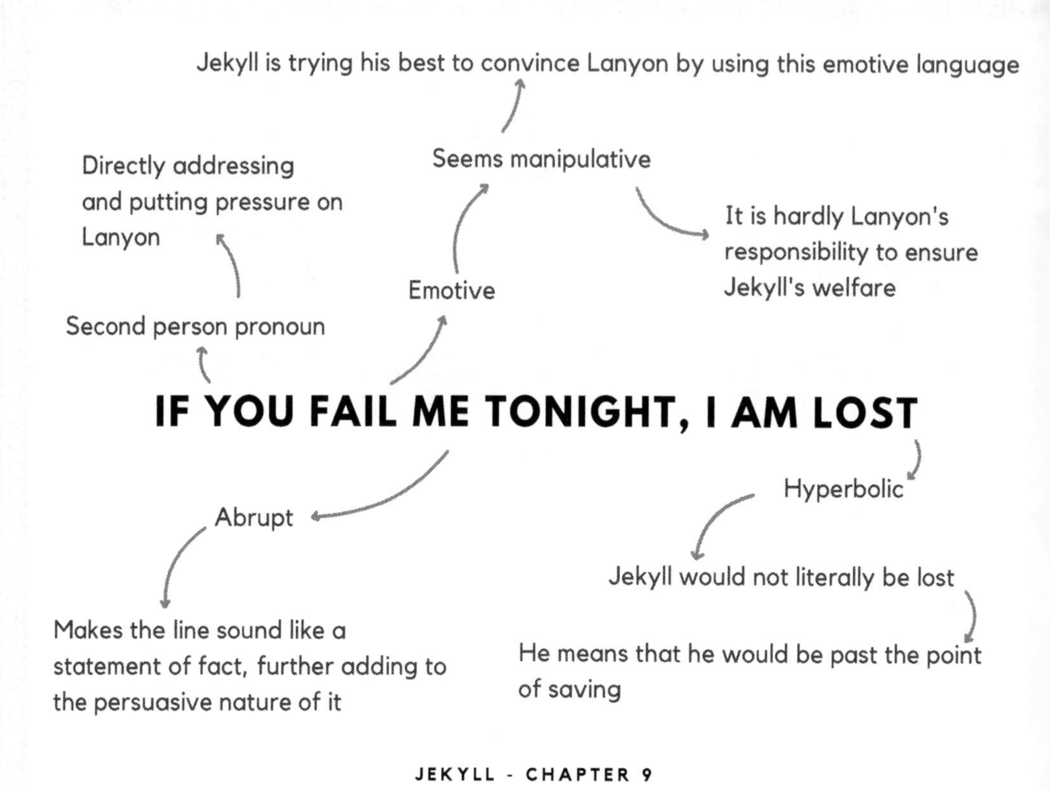

JEKYLL - CHAPTER 9

LINKS

Jekyll's reliance on Lanyon here contrasts with the earlier depiction of their strained, tense relationship.

Links to Lanyon's negative reaction to Utterson mentioning Jekyll's name in Chapter 6. At that point in the text, we don't understand why Lanyon reacts so strongly; we only learn in this letter that Lanyon witnessed Hyde transforming into Jekyll.

CONTEXT

Friendship was valued in Victorian times, particularly among the upper classes. Friendships were seen as a way of forming important connections and alliances, and those in the upper classes often sought out friendships with people whom they could benefit from economically, politically or socially. Here, Jekyll is trying to use his friendship with Lanyon to save himself from the scandal of being discovered to be Hyde.

THEMES / CHARACTERS

Hyde
Lanyon
Societal expectations
Reputation
Suspicion

SUMMARY

Lanyon, despite his suspicions, does as Jekyll asks. He takes a revolver with him, just in case. A man he has never met before enters and speaks with him informally. Lanyon, taken aback by the rudeness of the man, questions his behaviour.

Shows that he is a proper gentleman and respectable individual

Despite the strangeness of the situation, Lanyon had not forgotten his manners

This makes us more empathetic towards him, as he is a good character and does not deserve to be caught up in Jekyll's experiments

Polite

YOU FORGET THAT I HAVE NOT YET THE PLEASURE OF YOUR ACQUAINTANCE

Traditional expression

Formal language

In this case, it is definitely not a "pleasure"

Highlights the fact that he has never met Mr Hyde before as he is being very formal and polite

The ironic use of "pleasure" adds tension to the moment

LANYON - CHAPTER 9

LINKS

In Chapter 2, Hyde also lacked manners when Utterson tried to speak with him as he was trying to open the door to the back of Jekyll's house. Then, Hyde refused to look at Utterson and called him a liar before suddenly disappearing inside the house.

CONTEXT

Victorians lived in a time of great social change, and strict social customs were enforced. Etiquette was of the utmost importance and it was considered unacceptable to address someone without first being properly introduced. To have good manners was seen as a sign of respectability and class.

THEMES / CHARACTERS

Hyde
Lanyon
Suspicion
Curiosity
Supernatural
Deformity

SUMMARY

The man revealed that he was Mr Hyde. He explained that Lanyon had two options: Hyde could leave the place now with the potion and Lanyon would be none the wiser as to why Jekyll had asked him to do this, or Hyde could stay and show Lanyon the effects of the potion.

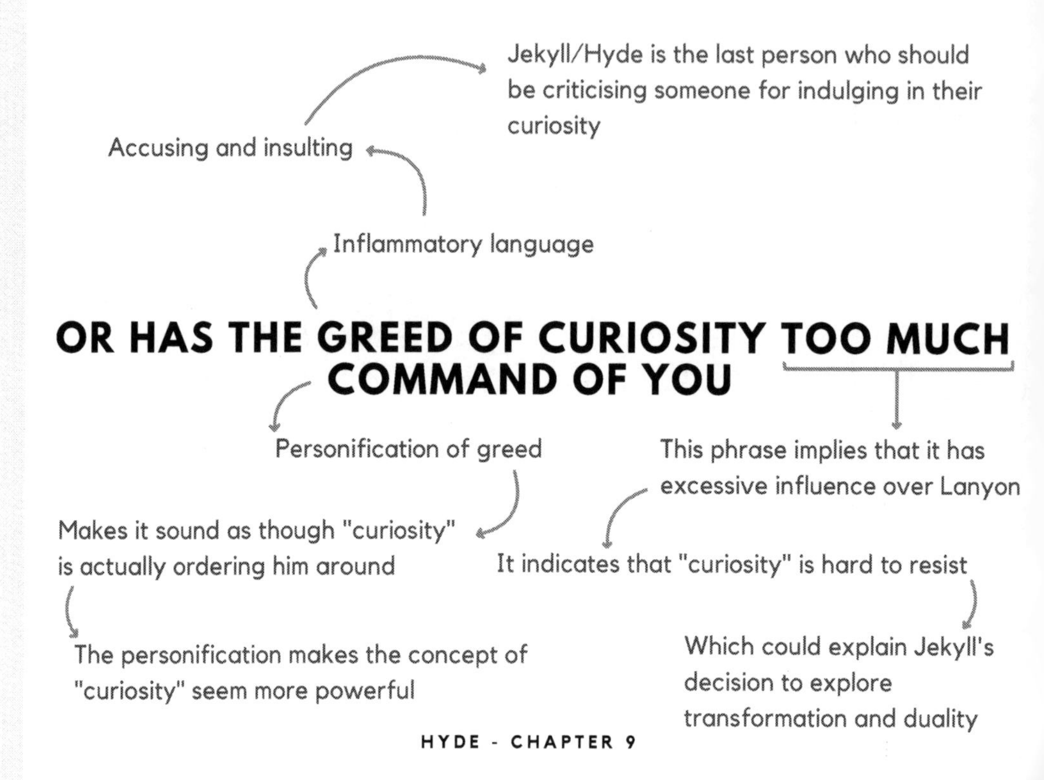

LINKS

This is ironic, as Jekyll's own curiosity has been the root cause of the issues in the text. It led him to investigate ways to explore his darker and more selfish side.

Links to Utterson's struggle to control his curiosity regarding Jekyll's relationship with Hyde.

CONTEXT

The use of the word "greed" indicates Hyde is critical of Lanyon's curiosity as, biblically speaking, greed is one of the seven deadly sins. Hyde is being hypocritical here, as his own curiosity drove him to explore the possibility of transformation. Lanyon has only become involved in this situation because Jekyll asked for his help.

THEMES / CHARACTERS

Hyde
Jekyll
Deformity
Supernatural
Science
Deception

SUMMARY

Lanyon decided to stay to witness the effects of the potion. He watched in horror as Hyde transformed into Jekyll. This quote describes Jekyll immediately after the transformation.

This mirrors the painful transformation

Makes the list appear laboured and difficult

This could make the reader consider the mental effects of the change on Jekyll

The transformation is described in physical terms

Syndetic listing

PALE AND SHAKEN, AND HALF FAINTING, AND GROPING BEFORE HIM WITH HIS HANDS, LIKE A MAN RESTORED FROM DEATH

Another interpretation could be that this is a religious reference to the resurrection of Jesus

Simile

Shows the physical impact the transformations are having on Jekyll

This could be seen as ironic, as Hyde is the personification of evil and thus not comparable to holy figures

This explains Jekyll's ill health later

LANYON - CHAPTER 9

LINKS

Other moments of transformation in the text include Jekyll previously having gone from being a recluse to having his social life "restored".

After witnessing Hyde transform into Jekyll, Lanyon's health rapidly declined and he was described in a similar manner to the way he described Jekyll in this quote post-transformation.

CONTEXT

The Victorian readers, being largely Christian, would have been familiar with the biblical story of Jesus's resurrection. On the third day after Jesus had been crucified and buried in a tomb, he was restored to life. Lanyon's reference here to "a man restored from death" could evoke ideas of the resurrection of Jesus; however, Jekyll's transformation was decidedly unholy.

THEMES / CHARACTERS

Jekyll
Hyde
Good vs Evil
Science
Societal expectations
Reputation

SUMMARY

Jekyll's account, found after his death, reveals his thoughts behind the experiment. He believed that society forces people to behave in a certain way, and that by nature, man is actually divided into two parts: a good side and a bad side.

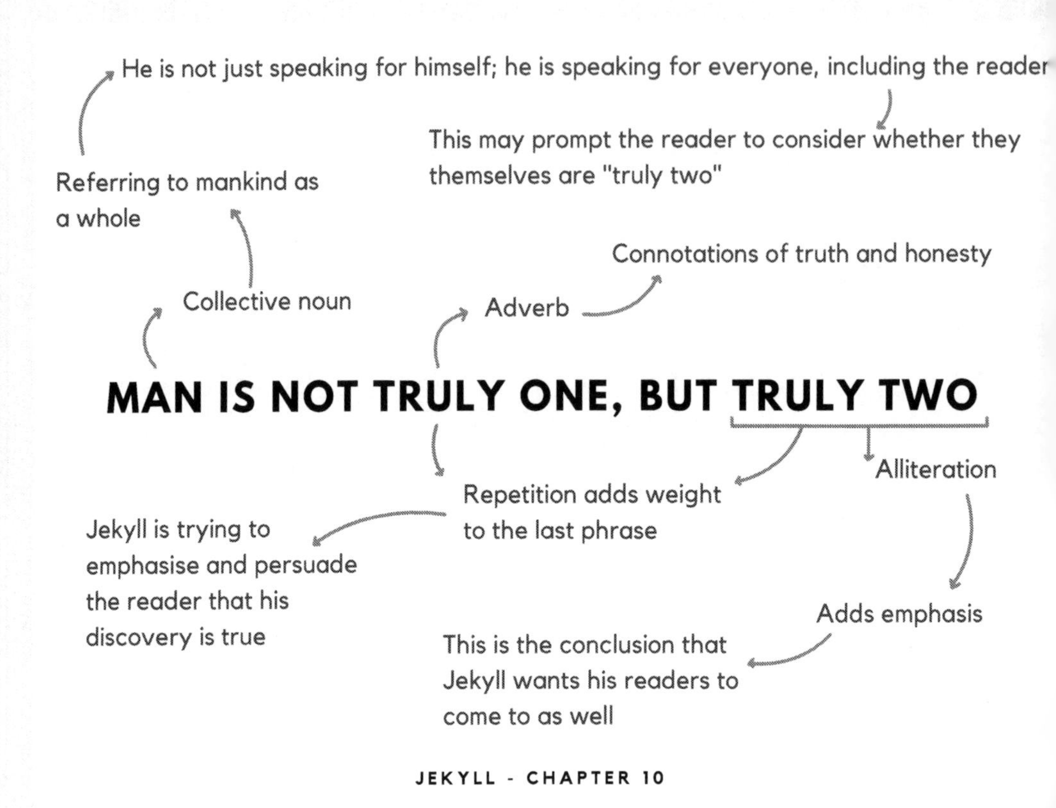

JEKYLL - CHAPTER 10

LINKS

Links to the theme of duality, which runs throughout the text.

While Jekyll and Hyde are the most significant examples of duality, there are others. Another example is the contrasting characters of the doctors. Dr Lanyon is an honest and "natural" scientist and doctor, while Dr Jekyll is an experimental, rule-breaking and unnatural one.

CONTEXT

Freud's *Structural Theory of the Mind* suggested that a person's mind was composed of the id, the ego, and the superego. The id contained more primitive, violent desires, the superego showed one's moral compass, and the ego was a balance of both. This division of personality, when balanced by the ego, is normal and non-destructive. Yet, Hyde is seemingly controlled by the id and is focused solely on violence and his own self-interest.

THEMES / CHARACTERS

Jekyll
Hyde
Science
Supernatural
Deformity

SUMMARY

Jekyll had decided to stop transforming into Hyde. Then one day, when he was sitting in a park, he suddenly noticed that his hand had changed; he had transformed into Hyde against his will and without taking the potion.

His attributes are not unique in themselves, but together and in extremes, they do make him stand out

Gives us a detailed understanding of Hyde's appearance

Listing

Could be seen as further evidence that Hyde is unnatural

Makes him sound unusually pale

LEAN, CORDED, KNUCKLY, OF A DUSKY PALLOR AND THICKLY SHADED WITH A SMART GROWTH OF HAIR

Means Hyde has thick hair

The emphasis on this phrase indicates that Hyde's arm is noticeably hairy

Not unusual in itself, but in addition to Hyde's "dwarfish", "beast-like" and "ape-like" characteristics, it does seem to create an odd appearance. Perhaps this is why no one can pinpoint the reason he looks "deformed"

JEKYLL - CHAPTER 10

LINKS

Links to descriptions of Hyde's animal-like qualities, such as his agility, strength, and tendency to act on instinct, as demonstrated in his attacks on Sir Danvers Carew and the child in Chapter 1.

Could also link to the idea of deformity that is so often associated with Hyde.

CONTEXT

The theory of atavism suggested that one could predict an individual's inclination towards good or evil based on their physical appearance. Those with more primitive features, such as large ears, a pronounced jaw, and a lot of body hair, were thought to be more likely to have criminal tendencies. In this passage, the description of the "smart", "thick" growth of hair on Hyde's hand indicates his primitive side and supports this theory of atavism.

THEMES / CHARACTERS

Jekyll
Hyde
Supernatural
Good vs Evil
Deformity
Science

SUMMARY

Jekyll realised with horror that he may no longer be in control of the situation. The supernatural effect of the potion had started to take over, causing him to transform randomly without meaning to.

This is not just a fear Jekyll has, but a scientific hypothesis

It sounds scientific and factual, which increases the tension

Reluctant to fully acknowledge the likelihood of this occurring

Formal language

Tentative language

THE BALANCE OF NATURE MIGHT BE PERMANENTLY OVERTHROWN, THE POWER OF VOLUNTARY CHANGE BE FORFEITED

Highlights the fact that this transformation was initially chosen by Jekyll, through his own free will

The same idea is repeated

Gives us the sense that he is trying to come to terms with it himself

Gives a sense of permanence which further adds to the tension

JEKYLL - CHAPTER 10

LINKS

The balance of nature is indeed overthrown as Jekyll begins to lose control over his transformations. An example that shows he has lost control is when he suddenly transforms into Hyde when speaking with Utterson and Enfield through his window.

Eventually, Jekyll loses the ability to stay in the form of Jekyll altogether.

CONTEXT

Gothic literature often focuses on the struggle between the natural and the unnatural (supernatural). The natural includes God, traditional values, and the natural environment. The unnatural includes themes like overt sexuality, excessive violence, and cruelty to innocents. Here, the natural is overpowered by the unnatural, which prevents Jekyll from controlling his transformations.

THEMES / CHARACTERS

Jekyll
Hyde
Good vs Evil
Supernatural
Societal expectations

SUMMARY

Jekyll decided that he would prefer to be stuck as Jekyll rather than Hyde. He quickly tried to conform to the previous restrictions of his life and reputation, but discovered that now that his evil side had been awakened, he could not return to his original goodness.

The positive connotations make Jekyll seem pleased to return to his previous way of life

An embrace is a sign of intimacy and affection

Reiterates the idea that Jekyll previously led a normal life

Makes his character more unsettling as the implication is that this could happen to anyone

Means 'again'

I EMBRACED ANEW THE RESTRICTIONS OF NATURAL LIFE

Contrast to his previous "unnatural" way of living through Hyde

Negative connotations

This implies that, despite enjoying the return to normality, Jekyll still believes that this way of living has its disadvantages

JEKYLL - CHAPTER 10

LINKS

Utterson is a clear example of a man who has lived a life full of "restrictions". He constantly has to try and suppress his suspicions and behave in a manner befitting his social status. Yet, ultimately, the text proves that this acceptance of social restrictions is preferable to the transgressions that lead Jekyll to his terrible fate.

CONTEXT

Victorian social standards and expectations were restrictive. This was part of the reason why Gothic texts became so popular; they allowed the repressed Victorians to indulge in ideas that would have been shocking for the time. The negative repercussions Jekyll faced could suggest that Stevenson was trying to warn his readers against resisting the restrictions of Victorian life.

BLANK QUOTE WORKSHEETS

THEMES / CHARACTERS

SUMMARY

“

”

SAID BY

LINKS

CONTEXT

THEMES / CHARACTERS

SUMMARY

“ ”

SAID BY

LINKS

CONTEXT

THEMES / CHARACTERS

SUMMARY

“

”

SAID BY

LINKS

CONTEXT

THEMES / CHARACTERS

SUMMARY

“ ”

SAID BY

LINKS

CONTEXT

THEMES / CHARACTERS

SUMMARY

“

”

SAID BY

LINKS

CONTEXT

THEMES / CHARACTERS

SUMMARY

“ ”

SAID BY

LINKS

CONTEXT

THEMES / CHARACTERS

SUMMARY

“

”

SAID BY

LINKS

CONTEXT

THEMES / CHARACTERS

SUMMARY

“ ”

SAID BY

LINKS

CONTEXT

THEMES / CHARACTERS

SUMMARY

“ ”

SAID BY

LINKS

CONTEXT

THEMES / CHARACTERS

SUMMARY

“ ”

SAID BY

LINKS

CONTEXT

THEMES / CHARACTERS

SUMMARY

“ ”

SAID BY

LINKS

CONTEXT

THEMES / CHARACTERS

SUMMARY

“

”

SAID BY

LINKS

CONTEXT

THEMES / CHARACTERS

SUMMARY

“ ”

SAID BY

LINKS

CONTEXT

THEMES / CHARACTERS

SUMMARY

“ ”

SAID BY

LINKS

CONTEXT

THEMES / CHARACTERS

SUMMARY

“ ”

SAID BY

LINKS

CONTEXT

THEMES / CHARACTERS

SUMMARY

“ ”

SAID BY

LINKS

CONTEXT

THEMES / CHARACTERS

SUMMARY

“ ”

SAID BY

LINKS

CONTEXT

THEMES / CHARACTERS

SUMMARY

“ ”

SAID BY

LINKS

CONTEXT

THEMES / CHARACTERS

SUMMARY

“ ”

SAID BY

LINKS

CONTEXT

THEMES / CHARACTERS

SUMMARY

“

”

SAID BY

LINKS

CONTEXT

PRACTICE QUESTIONS

QUESTION 1

Read the following extract from Chapter 1 (Story of the Door) of *The Strange Case of Dr Jekyll and Mr Hyde* and then answer the question that follows.

In this extract, Enfield tells Utterson about a violent incident he witnessed that has a connection to the door they have just passed on their walk.

Well, it was this way," returned Mr Enfield: "I was coming home from some place at the end of the world, about three o'clock of a black winter morning, and my way lay through a part of town where there was literally nothing to be seen but lamps. Street after street and all the folks asleep—street after street, all lighted up as if for a procession and all as empty as a church—till at last I got into that state of mind when a man listens and listens and begins to long for the sight of a policeman. All at once, I saw two figures: one a little man who was stumping along eastward at a good walk, and the other a girl of maybe eight or ten who was running as hard as she was able down a cross street. Well, sir, the two ran into one another naturally enough at the corner; and then came the horrible part of the thing; for the man trampled calmly over the child's body and left her screaming on the ground. It sounds nothing to hear, but it was hellish to see. It wasn't like a man; it was like some damned Juggernaut. I gave a few halloa, took to my heels, collared my gentleman, and brought him back to where there was already quite a group about the screaming child. He was perfectly cool and made no resistance, but gave me one look, so ugly that it brought out the sweat on me like running. The people who had turned out were the girl's own family; and pretty soon, the doctor, for whom she had been sent put in his appearance. Well, the child was not much the worse, more frightened, according to the sawbones; and there you might have supposed would be an end to it. But there was one curious circumstance. I had taken a loathing to my gentleman at first sight. So had the child's family, which was only natural. But the doctor's case was what struck me. He was the usual cut and dry apothecary, of no particular age and colour, with a strong Edinburgh accent and about as emotional as a bagpipe. Well, sir, he was like the rest of us; every time he looked at my prisoner, I saw that sawbones turn sick and white with the desire to kill him. I knew what was in his mind, just as he knew what was in mine; and killing being out of the question, we did the next best.

Starting with this extract, explore how Stevenson presents the theme of violence in *The Strange Case of Dr Jekyll and Mr Hyde*.

Write about:
- how Stevenson presents the theme of violence in this extract
- how Stevenson presents the theme of violence in the novel as a whole.

[30 marks]

THE PLAN

PARAGRAPH 1:

PARAGRAPH 2:

PARAGRAPH 3:

QUESTION 2

Read the following extract from Chapter 2 (Search for Mr Hyde) of *The Strange Case of Dr Jekyll and Mr Hyde* and then answer the question that follows.

In this extract, Utterson has decided to watch the entrance to Hyde's house in hopes of seeing him.

From that time forward, Mr Utterson began to haunt the door in the by-street of shops. In the morning before office hours, at noon when business was plenty and time scarce, at night under the face of the fogged city moon, by all lights and at all hours of solitude or concourse, the lawyer was to be found on his chosen post.

"If he be Mr Hyde," he had thought, "I shall be Mr Seek."

And at last his patience was rewarded. It was a fine dry night; frost in the air; the streets as clean as a ballroom floor; the lamps, unshaken by any wind, drawing a regular pattern of light and shadow. By ten o'clock, when the shops were closed, the by-street was very solitary and, in spite of the low growl of London from all round, very silent. Small sounds carried far; domestic sounds out of the houses were clearly audible on either side of the roadway; and the rumour of the approach of any passenger preceded him by a long time. Mr Utterson had been some minutes at his post, when he was aware of an odd light footstep drawing near. In the course of his nightly patrols, he had long grown accustomed to the quaint effect with which the footfalls of a single person, while he is still a great way off, suddenly spring out distinct from the vast hum and clatter of the city. Yet his attention had never before been so sharply and decisively arrested; and it was with a strong, superstitious prevision of success that he withdrew into the entry of the court.

The steps drew swiftly nearer, and swelled out suddenly louder as they turned the end of the street. The lawyer, looking forth from the entry, could soon see what manner of man he had to deal with. He was small and very plainly dressed and the look of him, even at that distance, went somehow strongly against the watcher's inclination. But he made straight for the door, crossing the roadway to save time; and as he came, he drew a key from his pocket like one approaching home.

Mr Utterson stepped out and touched him on the shoulder as he passed. "Mr Hyde, I think?"

Starting with this extract, explore how Stevenson presents the theme of curiosity in *The Strange Case of Dr Jekyll and Mr Hyde.*

Write about:

- how Stevenson presents the theme of curiosity in this extract
- how Stevenson presents the theme of curiosity in the novel as a whole.

[30 marks]

THE PLAN

PARAGRAPH 1:

PARAGRAPH 2:

PARAGRAPH 3:

QUESTION 3

Read the following extract from Chapter 4 (The Carew Murder Case) of *The Strange Case of Dr Jekyll and Mr Hyde* and then answer the question that follows.

In this extract, Utterson brings the police to Hyde's home, as they believe Hyde is responsible for the death of Sir Danvers Carew.

As the cab drew up before the address indicated, the fog lifted a little and showed him a dingy street, a gin palace, a low French eating house, a shop for the retail of penny numbers and twopenny salads, many ragged children huddled in the doorways, and many women of many different nationalities passing out, key in hand, to have a morning glass; and the next moment the fog settled down again upon that part, as brown as umber, and cut him off from his blackguardly surroundings. This was the home of Henry Jekyll's favourite; of a man who was heir to a quarter of a million sterling.

An ivory-faced and silvery-haired old woman opened the door. She had an evil face, smoothed by hypocrisy: but her manners were excellent. Yes, she said, this was Mr Hyde's, but he was not at home; he had been in that night very late, but he had gone away again in less than an hour; there was nothing strange in that; his habits were very irregular, and he was often absent; for instance, it was nearly two months since she had seen him till yesterday.

"Very well, then, we wish to see his rooms," said the lawyer; and when the woman began to declare it was impossible, "I had better tell you who this person is," he added. "This is Inspector Newcomen of Scotland Yard."

A flash of odious joy appeared upon the woman's face. "Ah!" said she, "he is in trouble! What has he done?"

Mr Utterson and the inspector exchanged glances. "He don't seem a very popular character," observed the latter. "And now, my good woman, just let me and this gentleman have a look about us."

Starting with this extract, explore how Stevenson creates mystery and tension in *The Strange Case of Dr Jekyll and Mr Hyde.*

Write about:
- how Stevenson creates mystery and tension in this extract
- how Stevenson creates mystery and tension in the novel as a whole.

[30 marks]

THE PLAN

PARAGRAPH 1:

PARAGRAPH 2:

PARAGRAPH 3:

QUESTION 4

Read the following extract from Chapter 6 (Incident of Dr Lanyon) of *The Strange Case of Dr Jekyll and Mr Hyde* and then answer the question that follows.

In this extract Utterson, after attempting to see Jekyll for two months without success, goes to Lanyon's residence and is granted entry.

The rosy man had grown pale; his flesh had fallen away; he was visibly balder and older; and yet it was not so much these tokens of a swift physical decay that arrested the lawyer's notice, as a look in the eye and quality of manner that seemed to testify to some deep-seated terror of the mind. It was unlikely that the doctor should fear death; and yet that was what Utterson was tempted to suspect. "Yes," he thought; "he is a doctor, he must know his own state and that his days are counted; and the knowledge is more than he can bear." And yet when Utterson remarked on his ill looks, it was with an air of great firmness that Lanyon declared himself a doomed man.

"I have had a shock," he said, "and I shall never recover. It is a question of weeks. Well, life has been pleasant; I liked it; yes, sir, I used to like it. I sometimes think if we knew all, we should be more glad to get away."

"Jekyll is ill, too," observed Utterson. "Have you seen him?"

But Lanyon's face changed, and he held up a trembling hand. "I wish to see or hear no more of Dr Jekyll," he said in a loud, unsteady voice. "I am quite done with that person; and I beg that you will spare me any allusion to one whom I regard as dead."

"Tut, tut!" said Mr Utterson; and then after a considerable pause, "Can't I do anything?" he inquired. "We are three very old friends, Lanyon; we shall not live to make others."

"Nothing can be done," returned Lanyon; "ask himself."

"He will not see me," said the lawyer.

"I am not surprised at that," was the reply. "Some day, Utterson, after I am dead, you may perhaps come to learn the right and wrong of this. I cannot tell you. And in the meantime, if you can sit and talk with me of other things, for God's sake, stay and do so; but if you cannot keep clear of this accursed topic, then in God's name, go, for I cannot bear it."

Starting with this extract, explore how Stevenson presents the theme of transformation in *The Strange Case of Dr Jekyll and Mr Hyde*.

Write about:

- how Stevenson presents the theme of transformation in this extract
- how Stevenson presents the theme of transformation in the novel as a whole.

[30 marks]

THE PLAN

PARAGRAPH 1:

PARAGRAPH 2:

PARAGRAPH 3:

QUESTION 5

Read the following extract from Chapter 8 (The Last Night) of *The Strange Case of Dr Jekyll and Mr Hyde* and then answer the question that follows.

In this extract, Poole attempts to show Utterson Jekyll's odd behaviour. He knocks on Jekyll's door and pretends that Utterson wants to see Jekyll.

Mr Utterson's nerves, at this unlooked-for termination, gave a jerk that nearly threw him from his balance; but he recollected his courage and followed the butler into the laboratory building through the surgical theatre, with its lumber of crates and bottles, to the foot of the stair. Here Poole motioned him to stand on one side and listen; while he himself, setting down the candle and making a great and obvious call on his resolution, mounted the steps and knocked with a somewhat uncertain hand on the red baize of the cabinet door.

"Mr Utterson, sir, asking to see you," he called; and even as he did so, once more violently signed to the lawyer to give ear.

A voice answered from within: "Tell him I cannot see anyone," it said complainingly.

"Thank you, sir," said Poole, with a note of something like triumph in his voice; and taking up his candle, he led Mr Utterson back across the yard and into the great kitchen, where the fire was out and the beetles were leaping on the floor.

"Sir," he said, looking Mr Utterson in the eyes, "Was that my master's voice?"

"It seems much changed," replied the lawyer, very pale, but giving look for look.

"Changed? Well, yes, I think so," said the butler. "Have I been twenty years in this man's house, to be deceived about his voice? No, sir; master's made away with; he was made away with eight days ago, when we heard him cry out upon the name of God; and who's in there instead of him, and why it stays there, is a thing that cries to Heaven, Mr Utterson!"

"This is a very strange tale, Poole; this is rather a wild tale my man," said Mr Utterson, biting his finger. "Suppose it were as you suppose, supposing Dr Jekyll to have been—well, murdered, what could induce the murderer to stay? That won't hold water; it doesn't commend itself to reason."

Starting with this extract, explore how Stevenson creates an atmosphere of tension in *The Strange Case of Dr Jekyll and Mr Hyde.*

Write about:

- how Stevenson creates an atmosphere of tension in this extract
- how Stevenson creates an atmosphere of tension in the novel as a whole.

[30 marks]

THE PLAN

PARAGRAPH 1:

PARAGRAPH 2:

PARAGRAPH 3:

WRITING TIPS

EXAMPLE ESSAY STRUCTURE

There are many different ways to structure an essay. There is not one single way that works for every essay. Find a structure that you feel confident working with and adapt it to the question's needs. Below is a generic essay structure with some tips on what to include.

INTRODUCTION

Topic sentence using the wording of the question.

List of points you are going to make in the body of your essay.

MAIN BODY

Try to aim for 3-4 PEEL paragraphs.

If you are given an extract question try to divide your essay up equally, so half the essay is based on the extract and half is based on the play as a whole.

Make sure you spend time analysing your quotations fully. The best way to get great marks is to analyse quotes in-depth and provide alternative interpretations.

Don't forget to include context!

CONCLUSION

Link the points you have made in the body of your essay to the question.

Write a brief concluding thought on the question.

PEEL PARAGRAPH STRUCTURE

POINT

A short sentence at the beginning of your paragraph detailing the point you are about to make. Students often find it helpful to use the wording of the question in the point - though remember to relate it to the specific topic you are going to cover in your paragraph.

EVIDENCE

This is the quotation that you will use to support your point. It is best to keep the actual quote as short as possible - make sure you only include what you are going to break down and analyse.

EXPLAIN

Here you want to explain how your quotation relates to your point. Try to use close word analysis or literary technique analysis to uncover meaning in the text. You can also consider different interpretations and the effects of those interpretations. It is a good idea to include relevant context here. This should be the largest part of your paragraph.

LINK

Make sure you round off your point and clearly link it to the question. This is a good place to check you are actually answering the question fully.

EXAMPLE PARAGRAPH

EXPLORE HOW STEVENSON PRESENTS THE THEME OF EVILNESS IN *THE STRANGE CASE OF DR JEKYLL AND MR HYDE.*

Point: Stevenson presents the theme of evilness as intrinsically linked to the animalistic physicality of Mr Hyde.

Evidence: We can see this in the quote "[l]ean, corded, knuckly, of a dusky pallor and thickly shaded with a smart growth of hair".

Explain: The use of listing emphasises the number of primitive characteristics that Hyde possesses, making him appear more animal than human. This lack of humanity contributes to the atmosphere of evilness that allegedly surrounds Hyde according to those whom he encounters. The phrase "dusky pallor" is evocative of pale, sickly skin. This could perhaps suggest that evil is essentially an illness, something that is contagious that can alter the appearance of the afflicted. Or, the "pallor" could simply be the result of the lack of sun due to Jekyll's social isolation. The phrase "smart growth of hair" indicates the thick body hair Hyde possesses, which is reminiscent of an animal. Contextually, atavism was a popular theory; it suggested that you could predict an individual's inclination towards good or evil based on their physicality. Those who appeared more primitive, with large ears or a pronounced jaw or a lot of body hair, were seen as more likely to have criminal tendencies. Hyde's physical hairiness signals his primal nature, and thus his propensity to evil inclinations. His animal-like physicality is also linked to evilness through the quote "ape-like fury". The simile comparison to an ape is made when Hyde brutally attacks and beats Sir Danvers Carew to death. The violence of the act is associated with the primitive, aggressive "ape".

Link: Ultimately, Stevenson presents evilness as an abhorrent regression to a more primitive animalistic state, the antithesis of everything a good, stereotypical Victorian gentleman would strive to emulate.

GLOSSARY OF LITERARY TECHNIQUES

GLOSSARY OF LITERARY TECHNIQUES

ALLITERATION

The repetition of the same consonant sound, especially at the beginning of words.

ALLUSION

A reference to another event, person, place or work of literature. The allusion is usually implied rather than explicit and provides another layer of meaning to what is being said.

ANTAGONIST

A character that is the source of conflict in a literary work.

ASIDE

A dramatic device in which a character makes a short speech intended for the audience but not heard by the other characters on stage.

ASYNDETIC LISTING

When words are joined without the use of a conjunction, but with commas instead

COLLOQUIAL

Ordinary, everyday speech and language. Often very informal.

CONNOTATION

An implication or association attached to a word or phrase.

DIALOGUE

Direct speech between characters in a literary work.

DICTION

Another word for "vocabulary". The choice of words a writer uses.

GLOSSARY OF LITERARY TECHNIQUES

DRAMATIC IRONY

Where the audience's or reader's understanding of events or individuals in a work surpasses that of its characters.

END STOPPING

A verse line with a pause or stop at the end of it.

ENJAMBMENT

A line of verse that flows on into the next line without a pause (comma or full stop).

FIGURATIVE LANGUAGE

Language that is symbolic or metaphorical and not meant to be taken literally.

FORESHADOWING

A warning or indication of a future event.

GENRE

A particular type or style of writing – eg prose, poetry, tragedy, romance.

HYPERBOLE

Exaggerating for effect – it is not meant to be taken literally e.g. dying of boredom.

IMAGERY

The use of words to create a picture or "image" in the mind of the reader. Images can relate to any of the senses, not just sight.

INTERNAL RHYME

Rhyming words within a line rather than at the end of lines.

GLOSSARY OF LITERARY TECHNIQUES

IRONY

It occurs where a word or phrase has one surface meaning but another contradictory meaning is implied.

PLOT

The sequence of events in a poem, play, novel or short story that make up the main storyline.

PROTAGONIST

The main character or speaker in a text.

PUN

A play on words that have similar sounds but quite different meanings.

RULE OF THREE (TRICOLON)

Tricolon is a rhetorical term that consists of three parallel clauses, phrases, or words, which happen to come in quick succession without any interruption.

RHYME SCHEME

The pattern of rhymes in a poem.

RHYTHM

The 'movement' of the poem as created through the meter and the way that language is stressed within the poem.

SATIRE

The highlighting or exposing of human failings or foolishness through ridiculing them.

GLOSSARY OF LITERARY TECHNIQUES

SEMANTIC FIELD

A term used to describe a group of words, all of which share a similar concept, theme or subject.

SIMILE

A comparison using the words 'like' or 'as' to make the description more vivid.

SOLILOQUY

A dramatic device in which a character is alone and speaks his or her thoughts aloud.

STEROTYPE

Standardised, conventional ideas about characters, plots and settings.

STRUCTURE

The way a poem or play or other piece of writing has been put together.

SYMBOL

Symbols present things which represent something else. Often a material object representing something abstract.

SYNTAX

The way in which sentences are structured.

THEME

The central ideas that a writer explores through a text.

GLOSSARY OF LITERARY TECHNIQUES

METAPHOR

A comparison of one thing to another to make the description more vivid. The metaphor actually states that one thing is literally another.

MONOLOGUE

Monologue is an extended continuous speech, delivered in front of other characters and often has great thematic importance.

MOTIF

A recurring feature of a literary work that is related to the theme.

ONOMATOPOEIA

The use of words whose sounds copies the thing or process they describe, e.g. Boom.

OXYMORON

Phrase that consists of two words immediately next to one another that are contradictory: "living dead".

PARADOX

A statement that seems contradictory but may reveal a truth.

PERSONIFICATION

The attribution of human feelings, emotions, or sensations to an inanimate object.

INDEX OF QUOTES

INDEX OF QUOTES

INDEX OF QUOTES

Printed in Great Britain
by Amazon

21487304R00050